THE
STEADFAST
TIN SOLDIER

To Cam
from G'mon Lill
Christmas 1994

For Aidan, Fionnuala and Aodhán

HBJ

Text copyright © 1986 by Naomi Lewis
Illustrations copyright © 1991 by Patrick Lynch

First published 1991 by Andersen Press Ltd.
First U.S. edition 1992

Library of Congress Cataloging-in-Publication Data
Andersen, H. C. (Hans Christian), 1805–1875.
The steadfast tin soldier/by Hans Christian Andersen; newly
translated by Naomi Lewis; illustrated by Patrick Lynch. —
1st U.S. ed.
p.   cm.
"Gulliver books."
Summary: The perilous adventure of a toy soldier who loves a
paper dancing girl culminates in tragedy for both of them.
ISBN 0-15-200599-4
[1. Fairy tales.   2. Toys—Fiction.] I. Lynch, Patrick James, ill.
II. Title.
PZ8.A542St   1992
[E]—dc20   91-29953

Printed in Italy

A B C D E

HANS CHRISTIAN ANDERSEN

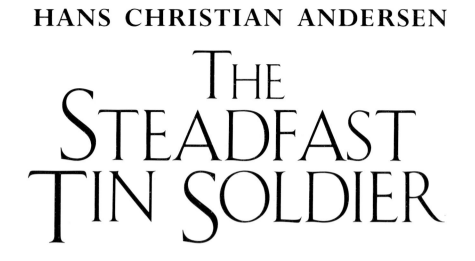

THE STEADFAST TIN SOLDIER

Newly translated from the Danish
by NAOMI LEWIS

Illustrated by

P. J. LYNCH

Gulliver Books

Harcourt Brace Jovanovich, Publishers

San Diego   New York   London

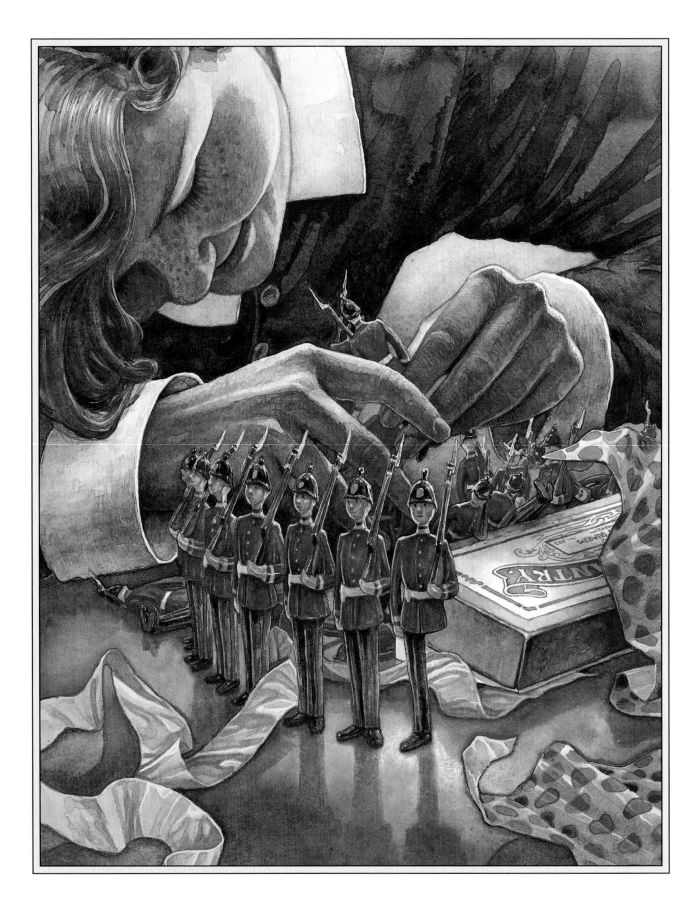

THERE were once twenty-five tin soldiers, all of them brothers, for they had been made from the same tin spoon. They shouldered muskets, stared straight ahead, and looked very handsome in their red and blue uniforms.

"Tin soldiers!" were the very first words they heard in this world when the lid of their box was taken off. A little boy had shouted those words and clapped his hands happily—he had been given the soldiers as a birthday present. He immediately set them up all in a row on the table. Each soldier was exactly like the next—except for one that only had a single leg. He was the last to be molded, and there wasn't enough tin left. Yet he stood just as well on his one leg as the others did on their two, and he is this story's hero.

On the table where they stood were many other toys, but the one everyone noticed first was a magnificent paper castle. Through its little windows you could see right into the rooms. In front of it tiny trees were arranged around a piece of mirrored glass that was meant to look like a lake. Swans made of wax seemed to float on its surface, gazing at their white reflections.

The whole scene was enchanting, but the prettiest thing of all was a girl who stood in the open doorway. She, too, was cut out of paper, but her gauzy skirt was of the finest muslin; a narrow blue ribbon crossed over her shoulder like a scarf and was held by a shining sequin almost as large as her face. This charming little lady held her arms stretched out, for she was a dancer — indeed, one of her legs was raised so high in the air that the tin soldier could not see it at all, and he thought that she had only one leg like himself.

She would be the perfect wife for me, he thought. But she is so grand! She lives in a castle, and I have only a box — and there are five-and-twenty of us in that! There certainly isn't room for her. Still, I can try to make her acquaintance. So he lay down behind a snuffbox that was on the table. From there he could easily watch the little paper dancer, who continued to stand on one leg without losing her balance.

When evening came, all the other tin soldiers were put in their box, and the children went to bed. Then the toys began to play games of their own — they visited each other, and pretended to go to school, and staged battles, and went to parties. The tin soldiers rattled in their box, for they wanted to join in, but they couldn't get the lid off. The nutcrackers turned somersaults, and the chalk squeaked on the chalkboard; there was so much noise that the canary woke up and took part in the playing and chattering — what's more, he spoke in verse. The only two who didn't move were the tin soldier and the little dancer. She continued to stand on the point of her toe, with her arms held out; he stood just as steadily on his single leg — and never once did he take his eyes off her.

Then the clock struck twelve. *Crack!* — the snuffbox lid flew open and up hopped a little black goblin. There was no snuff in the box — it was a kind of trick, a jack-in-the-box.

"Tin soldier!" screeched the goblin. "Keep your eyes to yourself!"

But the tin soldier pretended not to hear.

"All right, just you wait till tomorrow!" said the goblin.

When morning came and the children were up again, the tin soldier was placed on the windowsill. The goblin may have been responsible, or perhaps a breeze blowing through the room — in any case, the window suddenly swung open, and out fell the tin soldier, three stories to the ground. It was a frightful fall! His leg pointed upward, his head down, and he landed with his bayonet stuck between two stones in the pavement.

The servant girl and the little boy went looking for him in the street, but although they almost stepped on the soldier they somehow failed to see him. If he had called out "Here I am!" they would have found him easily, but he didn't think it proper behavior to shout when he was in uniform.

Then it began to rain. The drops fell fast and soon turned into a drenching shower. When it was over, two boys came along. "Look!" said one. "There's a tin soldier. Let's send him out to sea."

So they made a boat out of newspaper and put the tin soldier in the middle, and set it in the fast-flowing water in the gutter at the edge of the street. Away he sped, and the two boys ran beside him clapping their hands. What waves there were in that gutter stream! What rolling tides! It had really poured down. The paper boat tossed up and down, sometimes spinning around and around until the soldier felt quite dizzy. But he remained as steadfast as ever, not moving a muscle, still looking straight ahead, still shouldering his musket.

All at once the boat entered a tunnel under the sidewalk. Oh, it was dark, as dark as it was in the box at home. Wherever am I going now? the tin soldier wondered. Yes, this must be the goblin's doing. Ah! If only that young lady were here with me in the boat, I wouldn't care if it were twice as dark.

Suddenly, from its home in the tunnel, a large water rat rushed out. "Have you got a passport?" it demanded. "No entry without a passport!"

But the tin soldier didn't say a word; he only gripped his musket more tightly than ever. The boat rushed onward, with the rat rushing after it, grinding its teeth. It yelled to the sticks and straw, "Stop him! Stop him! He hasn't paid his toll! He hasn't shown his passport!"

There was no stopping the boat, though, for the stream ran stronger and stronger. The tin soldier could just see a bright glimpse of daylight far ahead where the end of the tunnel must be, but at the same time he heard a roaring noise which might well have frightened a braver man. Just imagine! At the end of the tunnel the stream thundered down into a great canal. It was as dreadful for him as a plunge down a giant waterfall would be for one of us.

But how could he stop? Already he was close to the edge. The boat raced on, and the poor tin soldier held himself as stiffly as he could—no one could say of him that he even blinked an eye. Suddenly the little vessel whirled around three or four times and filled with water right to the brim—what could it do but sink! The tin soldier stood in water up to his neck.

Deeper and deeper sank the boat, softer and softer grew the paper, until at last the water closed over the soldier's head. He thought of the lovely little dancer whom he would never see again, and in his ears rang the words of a song:

Onward, onward, warrior brave!
Fear not danger, nor the grave.

Then the paper boat collapsed entirely. The tin soldier fell out and was promptly swallowed by a fish.

Oh, how dark it was in the fish's stomach! It was even worse than the tunnel, and much more cramped. But the tin soldier's courage remained unchanged: there he lay, as steadfast as ever, his musket still at his shoulder. The fish thrashed wildly about, twisted and turned, and then became still. Some time later, something flashed through like a streak of lightning — then all around was cheerful daylight, and a voice cried out, "The tin soldier!" The fish had been caught, taken to market, sold, and carried into the kitchen, where the cook had cut it open with a large knife. She picked up the soldier, holding him around his waist with her finger and thumb, and took him into the living room, so that the whole family could see the remarkable character who had traveled inside of a fish.

But the tin soldier was not at all proud. They stood him up on the table, and there — well, the world is full of wonders! — he saw that he was in the very same room where his adventures had started. There were the very same children and the very same toys, and there was the fine paper castle with the graceful little dancer at the door. She was still poised on one leg, with the other raised high in the air. Ah, she was steadfast, too. The tin soldier was deeply moved. He would have liked to weep tin tears, but that would not have been soldierly behavior. He looked at her, and she looked at him, but not a word passed between them.

And then a strange thing happened. One of the little boys picked up the tin soldier and threw him into the stove. He had no reason for doing this — it must have been the snuffbox goblin's fault.

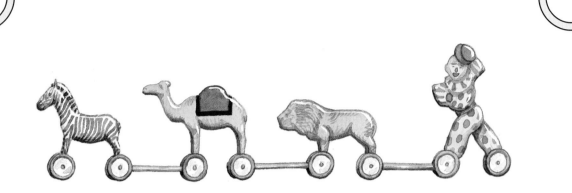

The tin soldier stood framed in a blaze of light. The heat was intense, but whether the heat came from the fire or his burning love, he could not tell. And his bright colors were now gone — but whether they had been washed away by his journey, or by his grief, none could say. He looked at the pretty little dancer, and she looked at him. He felt that he was melting away, but he still stood steadfast, shouldering his musket. Suddenly the door flew open, a gust of air caught the little paper girl, and she flew like a sylph right into the stove, straight to the waiting tin soldier. There she flashed into flame and vanished.

The soldier soon melted down to a lump of tin, and the next day, when the maid raked out the ashes, she found him in the shape of a little tin heart. And the dancer? All they found was her sequin and that was as black as soot.